Joyce to the World

A collection of short es

inspired by Joyce Grenfell

By Sarah Miller Walters

A History Usherette Book

Original Text © Sarah Miller Walters 2016

Cover Artwork © Howard Taylor 2016

Introduction

Joyce Grenfell died in 1979, just before she was due to become Dame Joyce Grenfell. But she is by no means forgotten, indeed she is thought of fondly by many of us who are too young to have been aware of her during her lifetime. It is interesting to think about the reasons for this, when many of her contemporaries are becoming more obscure as time passes.

The two roles that she is most fondly remembered for are Policewoman Ruby Gates in the St Trinian's films; and the harassed nursery school teacher as portrayed in her monologues. Indeed, mention Joyce's name to a lot of people and they will smile and reply "George, don't do that!" These characters have similarities – at first glance they are failures.

Ruby fails to secure marriage with her long-term fiancé Sammy and she is hopeless at controlling the school girls while masquerading as a games mistress. The nursery school teacher loves children but it is not returned in the fashion that she probably envisaged. But, we British love an underdog, especially one that perseveres to the point of insanity. Of course it helps when they have a hilarious turn of phrase too. We adore Joyce as a character that has been lost to progress, to dumbing down and mass boorishness. She represents an England that we feel we have left behind.

But Joyce herself was half American and she was no underdog. The world that she represents to many of us did not exist in the pure form that we sometimes imagine either.

In my blog, The History Usherette, I look at nostalgic films and try to pick out pieces of real history. This history is often not as rose-tinted as we would like it to be. I have applied this thought to this collection of short stories. Each is inspired by a piece of Joyce's work, they run in chronological order from the 1930s to the 1970s. I hope – and I think that Joyce might approve of this – that this might encourage the reader to appreciate some the progress that we have made in more recent decades. It is fun to look back and think that maybe things were better. But they weren't. Not always.

Natures Gifts:

The original speaker of 'Useful and Acceptable Gifts', first performed by Joyce in revue in the 1930s, is horrified to see herself being parodied on stage. Many women remained single into middle and old age at this point in time due to the mass slaughter of young men in World War One. Yet to be married and a mother was still looked upon as a woman's only natural calling. Those that tried to make themselves useful in other ways were sometimes turned into figures of fun.

The Demi-Angel:

Upper class teenager Julia volunteers to help care for wounded soldiers in 1943, going against her mother's wishes. She is inspired after watching Joyce in the film 'The Demi Paradise'.

A rigid class system and narrow constraints for women was to some extent broken down by World War Two. This is a look at how it took death and injury on a mass scale to liberate those trapped at home as well as those in the occupied territories.

Dear Miss Grenfell:

Old soldier Robert writes to Joyce to thank her for cheering him up while she was touring with ENSA. Like so many household names, it was this wartime work that really helped to shape Joyce into the performer we so loved. It took war to allow talent to shine through, and to introduce people to different forms of culture.

Red Letter Day:

Old bachelor Jim is haunted by Joyce's song 'I'm Going to See You Today.'

These 1940s lyrics paint a picture of a nation being reunited again with loved ones. It might refer to short leaves from the fighting, or to the post war homecoming. But the war took a huge toll on British relationships. Divorce rates were hitherto unheard of, and this is only the official picture. Some promised marriages didn't happen; while some unhappy marriages limped on to save face.

Oh Ruby!:
Billy's mother discusses his decision to join the police force.
We all love St Trinian's, although I think it does colour our perception of all-girl schools. Do we let what we see on screen influence our lives too much? Are we losing the capability to make decisions for ourselves?

Forgetting:
New husband Bob struggles to reconcile his views of marriage with a society where women are newly liberated. He tries to take back control, implementing

a hare-brained scheme inspired by Joyce's 'forgetful woman in church' monologue.

The laws are in place, but male attitudes are too often trailing behind. Even now, I wonder if we'll ever get true equality.

Some Ladies Have to Dance Together:
A woman reflects on how she first hated, then loved Joyce's song 'Stately as a Galleon.'
Another look at how girls are at the mercy of men's expectations, often rooted in their own base desires.

Retirement Time:
Joyce's nursery teacher dedicated her life to her job (although she often thought about a change of career, she could never quite break away). But when she reaches a certain age she is forced to retire with no other life to fill her days.

*****

Prologue - Walking With Joyce

I wanted to go to Aldeburgh for the holidays. I knew that a whole week there would never be stood by my family. Too quiet, not enough to do, they would say. I booked a caravan in Felixstowe for a week in August instead. When we were settled in, with all the seaside delights tasted, I suggested we took a drive up the coast. Take in the scenery, visit somewhere we hadn't seen before. It wasn't met with any enthusiasm. Only the guilt of the older members of the party got us in the car. Everyone else had done what they wanted to do. It was my turn to choose. The youngest couldn't understand why she was being taken from her little paradise of beach, shops and slot machines. She didn't want to be stuck in the car. She didn't want to go anywhere else.

"I hope Aldeburgh's not going to be another Southwold." The eldest sighed, recalling a long drive from Lowestoft a couple of years back. When we got to Southwold, it was too full of other people and there wasn't enough to actually do. He has to 'do' constantly, so that none of us are allowed the luxury (or I would say necessity) of sitting and watching the world turn. He races ahead to a burnt out future.

We parked by that famous shingled beach and walked into the town. A few steps along the pebbled banks and a brief fascination with Sizewell up the coast. I wanted to see the sculpture. I wanted to see Britten's house. But then the creature pulling on my right hand began to drag.

"I want to go back. I want to go back to Felixstowe NOW!"
The others were silent. We trudged along, our calves working the shingle. I became the frowned upon mother that shouts at her child in public. We ate an ill-tempered supermarket picnic, squashed onto a bench and looking out to an empty sea. At last I had to admit defeat and sanction a return to the car and the thrumming seaside resort that the others craved. I photographed as much as I could and wondered if

that time would come when I could return and join the serene set, just being, not doing.

In the meantime, Joyce can take me there when I pick up her books and letters. She can take me to Aldeburgh, to Cliveden and to London's theatreland. To picnics and bird-watching. To a time when, war aside, life didn't seem to demand as much from you as it does today. When attention spans were longer and our pleasures simpler.

Was it that good....?

Nature's Gifts

"You must come and see it!" they told her. She was in London, visiting her youngest brother and his wife. They were fond of culture; proud of the wide sweep of West End establishments that had benefited from their patronage. Every play, every revue, every concert – this appeared to be their sole aim. She wondered what would happen when the children came along. Would they eschew entertainment or would they abandon their offspring to the care of strangers? Despite this worry she did hope that they would have children. That aspect of life had been denied to her and so the prospect of being the kindly and fun Aunt seemed to be her only remaining option. She knew that she would be good with children. It was her ability to make things. She could transform anything into something either useful or beautiful, just as Ruskin himself had suggested. She envisaged collecting acorn cups from beneath the trees in Hyde Park with two young scamps, then taking them back to paint them gold and string them together into garlands.

Theatreland (she had seen that word on an underground poster and liked it) bustled. But the theatre that they took her into was intimate. It wasn't quite on the main drag; it nestled around a corner, squatting beneath the showy facades with familiar names. The programme listed only acts that were unfamiliar to her. She browsed through it, to try and find the flavour of the evening. Her brother and his wife settled themselves next to her, all expectant chuckles and arm touching. She half perched and awaited entertainment, her gloves in her lap and her handbag at her neatly crossed ankles. The lights dropped.

As the revue progressed, a comfortable smile rested itself on her face. But the fluidity of her lips was arrested as a lady called Joyce Grenfell began to recite her monologue. Up there on the stage she looked like her friend's grown up daughter, and so the cruelty that was to come was breathtaking. This so-called comic lecture on 'Useful and Acceptable Gifts' was much too familiar to be at all funny. She began to play with her gloves, so that her knuckles and veins became prominent. No-one had ever laughed when she delivered her lectures on how to make your own gifts. The ladies of the Womens' Institutes that she visited were always so pleased with her talks. Now here there was an entire theatre – absolutely full of people - simply hooting at another woman delivering what was practically one of her own speeches.

She began to mull over the most important facts. Was it this Grenfell's delivery that made it funny…or had people been sniggering behind their hands at her all of this time? What's more, had her brother and his wife deliberately brought her here to see this, knowing that someone had taken her work and somehow twisted it into a mocking parody? She took a sideways look at them. They were relaxed, laughing with their chins tilted delightedly at the stage. She went and powdered her nose, and took a very long time about it.

In the taxi, on the way back to their Westminster flat, they asked her for her thoughts.

"I say, you're a WI regular" her brother leaned towards her. "What did you think to the girl with her Useful and Acceptable Gifts? Are the talks really like that? I don't know how you keep yourself from laughing out loud!"

He and his wife chuckled, gazing at her steadily as the lights flashed by her face.

"Well, ah, yes. I suppose it was quite accurate. But somehow just not funny when you're in the church hall with the vicar's wife."

"Oh my dear!" Her brother patted her hand. "You are too funny!"

The Demi-Angel

Julia Hartsthorne had been born a few weeks early – eight months into her parents' marriage. She was a small baby, and prone to catch every illness doing the rounds of the nurseries. Her parents were rather high ranking members of the community, who believed in setting an example. Therefore, because of this rather hasty birth, they made much of her tiny size and weak constitution. They made sure that they told everyone that everything that was wrong with Julia was down to her being such an early baby – several times. There was no need for this really, because nobody thought for a minute that Julia's mother would have succumbed to the charms of any man before her wedding night. She was a famously uptight young woman, scathing in her disgust of modernity. Such was her lack of humour, there were some who thought it both just and amusing that her child should arrive so soon after her nuptials.

Julia had grown up swathed in the very expensive cotton wool of her mother's imagination, which effectively protected her from the nastiness outside of her very small world. After discovering the utter indignity of childbirth, her mother was reluctant to become pregnant again – consequently Julia's brothers were considerably younger than she was. Being so much used to her own company, she gave an impression of aloofness to others. However, far from being snobbish in her outlook (thanks to a happy choice of governess), Julia was simply deeply unsure of herself for much of her childhood.

By the time her age had moved into double figures, her initial delicacy had been thoroughly outgrown although she remained slight of stature and thin-haired. However, her mother so enjoyed the myth of her cocooned little survivor that she was reluctant to let it go. Julia was not allowed to go to school, a succession of governesses and tutors being brought to the house. Her mother also arranged a meagre social life too by inviting the children of her friends and acquaintances to play, regardless of whether the children could tolerate one another.

World War Two erupted when Julia was approaching her teenage years. At first, this was unsettling for her, as the army requisitioned her home in 1940. Her father took up a hush-hush post, working mostly in London while Julia and her mother and siblings had to move to a cottage on the edge of their estate. In recent years, because of the rather unsightly ribbon development of mock-Tudor bungalows, this cottage had become a definite part of the local village. The women of the village now turned to Julia's mother for leadership through their darkest days. She began to spend rather a lot of time away from the house running various associations and circles. Julia was told that she was too young to join the sewing circle when she tentatively asked if she might go along. Too much wifely gossip was the cryptic reason given. But she was allowed to stay in and knit socks for sailors, a monotonous and thankless task. Those that had called on her at the behest of their mothers had faded away too, bored by her lack of conversation.

Recognising this at least, Julia's mother confided in her daughter that she had become friendly with the local squire's wife, who had turned out to be the fourth daughter of Sir Barnaby Hardwicke. They had a daughter just a little older than Julia, and an invite to tea was being negotiated. One morning, she was told to expect an invite that very day. As the weather looked set to stay fine, she was permitted to walk to the manor, which was visible just beyond the church. This was with the proviso that she did not cross any fields.

Just before lunch, a postcard was presented to Julia. It was signed Agnes Redmond and it invited her to call in at the Manor at 3pm. Her expectations were not great. She rather hoped that she might fall ill before approximately 2.45, when she would have to set out for the manor house. She didn't mean to be anti-social but these people that her mother knew were always such bores. Ennui permeated everything that she did and she suspected that her life would only begin when her mother's ended.

On her arrival at the manor house, Julia's initial fears were realised. She was shown into a busy yet cosy looking room where Agnes sat in a tomato red sweater and dark slacks. She was welcomed in graciously yet informally – newspapers and knitting were removed hurriedly from the sofa. Julia sat and smoothed her tweed skirt over the baggy knees of her knitted stockings.

"Very glad to meet you, Miss Hartsthorne. I'll just call for tea."

"Oh please, Julia."

"Oh thank you. I'm Agnes, by the way."

"Yes. Very nice to meet you. Very nice of you to invite me."

"Well it was our mothers' idea really. But I am glad of the chance to make your acquaintance." Agnes leaned in and lowered her voice as a tired housekeeper brought the tea tray in. "You are such a mystery."

"Am I?"

Agnes nodded and began to pour from a silver tea pot. "We all know you exist, but we so rarely see you."

"No, well, I'm not allowed out very much. Only when the weather is fine."

"Why is that?"

"I was born too soon. I've always been small and sickly."

"I see. You look healthy today. I would say that your walk here has done you some good." Agnes handed Julia a cup of tea. "Sugar?"

"No thank you, I'm not allowed to have it at home so I've no taste for it."

"Well I never. There seems to be an awful lot that you're not allowed to do."

"I know. It's not so much that mother is strict, it's just that she worries so about me."

"Because you're so small? I suppose the rationing doesn't help, does it?"

Agnes smiled. Julia searched her face for as long as she dare. The smile did seem to be friendly rather than mocking which is what she had expected.

There was a pause, Julia stirred her sugarless tea.

"I don't feel all weak or ill, you know. It just seems that other people are determined that I am."

"Your mother does seem to be an..ah…determined lady."

Julia smiled and nodded.

"I suppose she lets you go to the cinema?"

"Ah, well, I have never been. But I've never asked to go, so I'm not sure whether I'm allowed or not."

"Never been!" Agnes clattered her cup and saucer onto the side table. "Never seen a film?"

"No, I don't believe that I have. But I have seen magazines with photographs of some of the film stars in. It all looks quite exciting."

"Oh you poor, poor thing!"

Julia blushed, she hadn't meant to sound so pathetic.

"Come on!" Agnes slapped her palms onto her thighs.
"I'm taking you."

"Taking me?"

"Yes, let's get the bus into Southbridge. I do believe that there is a Laurence Olivier showing. Have you seen his photograph?"

"Oh yes, I think I have!"

"Isn't he just a dream? Come on! We'll pay him a call." Agnes giggled Puckishly.

"Oh…well I haven't got a purse with me…"

"I'll pay this time – you can return the gesture next week when they've changed the film over."

Julia stood and wavered a little. Agnes took her hand and almost pulled her from the house towards the bus stop at the end of the lane.

"I'd guess that you've never been on a bus either." Agnes smiled as they settled onto the hot double seat near to the back. She slipped two coins into the conductress' hand.

"Two for Southbridge, please."

"Ta, ducky." The conductress winked at them both. "Have a nice time."

"How far is it to Southbridge?" Julia felt that she was almost shouting above the noise as the bus lumbered underneath the railway arch.

"It takes around ten minutes. We can get off right outside the Gaumont. Once we get inside, follow me to the best seats. We must be careful not to sit near any men, especially if they're in uniform. It's terrible the liberties they take.

Julia did all that Agnes bid, right up to the time that they were settled into the darkness. With Agnes on her left, and a tiny old lady with a large shopping bag on her right, she felt able to relax into the chair. It was a continuous programme and they had arrived in the middle of a newsreel. Julia saw the photographs that she had seen in newspapers and magazines, but now they moved and the narrative was spoken out loud. She was fixated, noiseless. Her jaw set firm. The feature film was called 'The Demi-Paradise' and it began after the news. Agnes leaned in and whispered

"It's good already, isn't it? Look, there he is, there's Laurence. Lovely."

Julia knew that this was something that she must do again. She could barely keep up with the story as new decisions flitted through her mind. It was time to join in with life. Her mother would insist that she risked illness, but now she knew that she had to counter-insist that everyone else risked their lives. She must volunteer to do something. But what could she do? She read, she poured tea, she knitted socks for sailors. She liked the character that first appeared on the bicycle, then later in the tea bar. She was young, organised, efficient…busy. These were words, Julia decided, that she wanted people to apply to herself; people who no longer viewed her a stranger. She had been hopelessly pleased at that wink from the bus conductress. She must reach out for more. Julia would become Sybil Paulson.

Her thoughts gushed over as she sat back on the bus. "I have to get out of the house, Agnes. What can I do? I want to volunteer."

"Oh yes, let's volunteer to do something together, it could be such fun." Agnes seemed to be infected by her joy in the idea.

"Is there something that we could do in Southbridge? Then we could come to the pictures afterwards."

"Splendid idea. Let's see…"
The bus stopped by the side of the cottage hospital. Three tired nurses climbed on, one of them taking the seat in front of Julia and Agnes. The pair looked at one another, then Agnes leaned over and tapped the nurse on the shoulder.
"Excuse me, Nurse, I'm sorry to trouble you but could you tell us if there's any voluntary work that we could do at the hospital?"
The nurse turned and looked them both over. "Oh, well, let's see…how old are you?"

"Sixteen." They spoke in unison.

"A bit young for helping on our wards, I'd say. I don't think our Matron would take you on. Have you tried Bickerton Lodge?"

"No. That's where the Parker-Finches live, isn't it?" Agnes knew very well that this was where Henry Parker-Finch had grown up. She had made it her business to know.

"It was." The nurse smiled. "It's a convalescent home for wounded servicemen at the moment. I believe that they need volunteers to dish out cups of tea, write letters to loved ones and so on. I expect that might suit you?"

"Wounded servicemen!" Both girls' minds exploded at the idea. Tall, handsome, airmen with slight limps; firm jawed naval officers with arms in slings.

The nurse giggled. "Yes, I can see that might suit very well."

"Mother would never let me do it." Julia turned to Agnes, her self -confidence ebbing away.

"Yes, I suppose mine might try and put a stop to it."

The nurse leaned a little further over the back of her seat. "Look, don't mention that it was my idea but I know the matron there. She's an extremely formidable lady and she will do anything to keep the staff and volunteers that she takes a liking to. And she knows how much visits mean to her men. Go and see matron first, if she likes you she'll take you on. If your parents kick up a fuss then get them to go and explain their misgivings to matron. I guarantee that they will come out of there utterly under her influence."

Agnes and Julia turned to each other "Shall we?" Agnes was uncertain, wondering quite what she'd led them both into. But Julia nodded vigorously; this might be her chance of escape from ennui.

"It's the next stop, you know." The nurse raised her eyebrows. Julia and Agnes stood and thanked her for her advice.

When they arrived at Bickerton Lodge it was matron's rest time. However, she agreed to see the girls in her rooms amongst a half-eaten afternoon tea. Behind her, on the wall, was a rather gaudy painting of the Virgin, and a sideboard beneath it displaying a half burned candle and a wilting bunch of wild flowers in a jam jar. Matron's gaze was steady, and she held it over each of the girls in turn. Julia, surprising herself, took the lead. She explained, quite humbly, she thought, that they were frustrated at being kept at home and wanted to do something more for the war effort.

Matron sucked her cheeks in momentarily. "Now listen, ladies." Her voice reminded Agnes of that rather silly Gracie Fields woman. "Yes I need help to read and write letters and dish out drinks. But I need help with the washing up and the floor mopping. What do you think to that?" She sat back and watched them both without blinking.

"Ah, well, we don't mind that either. Although I don't think we've ever done it before…" Julia looked at Agnes, who responded with a small shrug.

"Thought not." Matron looked satisfied to hear it. "We'll soon sort that out. And what do your mothers say?"

Julia was so surprised by the question that she answered truthfully. "We haven't told them."

"I see. Don't think they'll approve? Well, leave them to me. I don't bow and scrape, I tell them like it is. Any trouble, tell them to telephone." She wrote the number down briskly, tearing the corner of a discarded newspaper off. "Or they can call in and have a look at us. Otherwise I'll see you on Monday lunchtime. You can do the afternoons until rest time."

An old man in a tatty overall showed the girls to the door. He returned to Matron's room and poked his head around the door as she shovelled the remains of a sandwich into her mouth.
"Starry eyed new recruits eh?"
They shared a chuckle.

"The little mousy one might be good. She needs to do it for some reason. The other won't last five minutes."

"Flighty, you reckon?"

"Won't like being told what to do."

She let out a small belch behind her hand.

By the time Julia had arrived home her mother was preparing herself for dinner. "Julia, darling, where have you been until this time? I've sent Barker out to look for you. I presume that you got on well with Agnes?"

"Yes, mother. She took me to the cinema and we made a decision."

"The cinema!" Her string of pearls swung in mid-air. "Where! How!"

"We went on the bus to Southbridge."

"Tuberculosis! You will have picked up tuberculosis! Oh Julia! Why did you do it?" She sought a handkerchief among her dressing table drawer.

"But why will I have got some dreadful disease just by travelling a few miles on a bus?"

"Julia, workmen travel on buses and they spit."

"I didn't notice any. Anyway it's all rather beside the point, which is I have volunteered to help out at Bickerton Lodge. It's where injured servicemen are convalescing."

Julia's mother stood.

"I will be serving tea, reading letters and so on. I've been thinking, I might introduce poetry readings."

"I see."

"None of the men have anything contagious, mother. I'll be quite alright. Matron says that you can telephone her. She's very good. Religious."

"I see."

"If this war carries on any longer I'm probably going to be conscripted so I may as well start getting used to the work now."

"Never! You're far too delicate to be conscripted, Julia dear. Now if that's what is worrying you then there's no need…"

"Mother, there's nothing worrying me. I should be doing my bit for the brave boys and I'm going to start on Monday."

"But the socks…"

"There will still be time for socks."

"Well." Julia's mother sat down. "And how do you propose to get to Bickerton Lodge?"

"There's the bus. Or I could learn to cycle."

"Good lord!"

"I'd like to cycle, actually."

"I have no idea what your father is going to say."

"He told me that he drove a bus once in the General Strike, I expect he'll be rather proud."

Julia judged that to be the moment to retire to her room to change. She threw the window wide open and began to pin up her loose hair into a bun on the top of her head.

Dear Miss Grenfell

I hope you don't mind me writing to you like this after all this time. It's a good few years since we met, but we had such a good talk then that I felt sure you'd remember me. What with that and my injuries. I wasn't easy on the eye. I couldn't even look at myself in the mirror for months after I got blasted.

Just to remind you – it was 1944 in Italy. You came to the hospital to sing for us. I was so excited to see you because I knew of your work before the war. Just to know that you were coming was such a tonic. I expect a lot of the men told you that, but it is true. A real lady from dear old London, with a beautifully clear voice coming to sing just for us. We were like boys waiting for our birthday to come. You didn't let us down either, Miss Grenfell. A lovely mix of songs - some to remind us of home and some to make us smile. The chap in the bed next to me couldn't smile so he had to make do with shedding a couple of tears instead. He assured me in his funny way afterwards that these were tears of joy, and I believe him. When you had finished singing, you came around and chatted to us and spent a great deal of time on this. Some of those ENSA types flew in and flew straight back out again with barely a word for us. But you gave us all of your attention that evening. Then you saw me and settled down next to my bed for a good few minutes. I can't tell you how much that perked me up. Not just that I got special attention from you, but also because you didn't show any disgust at how I looked. If the singing job ever packs up, nursing is the job for you, dear Miss G! We had a very intimate chat, and I just couldn't help but pour my worries out to you. I told you that I was worried about how my wife would take to me when she finally saw me again. I had night terrors where she abandoned me for someone who hadn't had half his face blown off. You didn't fob me off, tell me that I didn't look that bad like one or two of the younger nurses did. But you told me truth that I was grateful for. You told me that if my wife was a decent woman who truly loved me then my injuries would make no difference. Otherwise, you said, perhaps I would do well to find another wife anyway! Common sense, of course. But I hadn't got much of that left and I am so grateful to you for showing me the way to go.

Well, now I'm all demobbed and the hospitals have done what they can. Thanks to a couple of decent surgeons things don't look too bad. But I wanted to share with you the joy I did find back home. My Doris has been the angel that I hoped she would be and we managed to pick up where we left off, just about. Not only that, we have a baby. I hoped and hoped for a little girl so we could name her Joyce. This time it was a boy though and we have called him Norman. But I won't stop until there is a girl! I'll let you know when little Joyce arrives.

Thank you.

Your servant,
Robert Davis.

Red Letter Day

As soon as the opening chords started up, Jim's mind abandoned the crossword altogether. Those few musical notes overrode any part of the present and swept him right back to Waterloo Station in late 1945. The vocals began…

"This is our red-letter day

It's come at last, you see."

Jim rose from his chair, his crossword pencil bouncing down onto the worn carpet and coming to rest by the electric-bar fire. He turned the radio off with a firm snap. Only the occasional click from the glowing electric bar sounded. But the action was a pointless one. He had heard enough to lodge the tune in his head…and those words that went with it. The words were the thing. They would nestle with him all evening. They may even linger on into the next day too. If it turned out to be a quiet week with nothing to snap its fingers at his brain – then it could last until next Sunday.

He had first heard the song when it was performed by Joyce Grenfell herself in the hospital. The injuries on his ward were relatively light, and all of the men paid rapt attention to her. The corporal in the next bed along had wanted to put some of the words in a letter to his wife – so Miss Grenfell had kindly dictated them out to him. The tune had been whistled and hummed all of the day after. As usual, Jim had laid back with his multiply fractured leg raised up, and had thought of Susie. What with the significance of the words, he began to associate the song with her, and his longing to see her again. He went over their last day together every night as he drifted into sleep…to see her again…that would be a red-letter day alright.

He heard the song performed again about a year later. He had listened to Bob Turner whistle it continually as he pinned photographs of his trio of girlfriends onto the wall above his bunk. And then it had played on the radio while he drunk his first beer on English soil. So, from boarding the train to London on that day he remembered too well, the song had been bumping around in his brain. The rhythm altered itself to fit the dominant noise of the moment, whether it was the sound of the train wheels, or the creaking of the carriage body as it pulled away from a platform. He caught a tube train from Kings Cross to Waterloo. He thought he could hear the tune in the wind as it rushed through the tunnels. She would be waiting for him at Waterloo, under the clock, of course. He had told her every time that they had met that this would be the place where it would all begin for them.

"We'll put our name down for a prefab, then get the marriage licence. When we've had our cup of tea and rock cake in the buffet. First thing's first."

This refreshment had become their ritual – at the beginning and end of each wartime liaison; a talisman. If they didn't have it, then perhaps one of them wouldn't return for next time. It was silly, they knew. But once the suggestion had been made it was difficult to let the idea go. He had smiled about it as he climbed the stairs up from the tube station onto the main concourse at Waterloo. This would be the last time. Now he was home, it would be all house hunting and picnics by the Serpentine.

Susie was already there. Others bunched around her, reading newspapers, checking the flapping indicator boards or looking hopefully into the crowds. Jim held up a hand in her direction, and called her name. She caught his eye and smiled. But it wasn't her usual smile. She pulled her gloves out of her handbag and put them on, even though the afternoon was mild. He reached her and took hold of her arm.

"What is it?"

"Let's go and get a cup of tea, shall we?" she smiled stiffly and his heart clenched a little bit more.

They moved through the crowd without speaking. They toured around piles of luggage before reaching the buffet on a tortuous route. As always, Susie went to find a seat for them both while Jim went to the counter. She touched his arm and nodded towards a table in the far corner.

"Just a tea for me please, Jim. No cake or anything."

He nodded as he felt in his pockets for coins. Somehow, he knew then that the wedding was off, and he sought a reason for this along with a sixpence. It must be something in the family, he decided. Her mother or father had fallen ill and she had to care for them. That must be the reason. He would tell her that needn't stop them from getting wed, they would find a way around it. Full of warmth at his own sense of compassion, he smiled benignly as he asked for two teas from the sour-faced girl behind the counter. He took the two weak teas to the table, swapping them around so that he got the one that had splashed into the saucer. He sat, and they looked at one another, each expecting the other to speak. Susie stirred her tea carefully, while Jim dabbed at the small brown pool in the saucer and moved his spoon about. He couldn't wait any longer.

"What is it, Susie?"

"I'm sorry Jim, really sorry."

And so, hesitantly, she told him what she was sorry for. That she had met another man whom she intended to marry. She had come to realise that war had changed them both, and that Jim was no longer the man for her. She didn't look at him. She finished her cup of tea while looking into the bottom of her cup for forgiveness. She was decided and would not change her mind. Not even give him a chance to find out for himself just how much the war had altered them.

Susie squeezed Jim's hand and they parted. "You'll find someone else, Jim. Someone is out there, just waiting to make you happy."
These were the final words that she ever spoke to him. She left him staring at nothing, with that song still in his head.
"A red letter day"
"I'll see you today."
But she was gone already.

Jim was a man of his word. He had promised himself to Susie, he would remain hers, always. Even when the other men in his unit had been sampling all the pleasures of the continent, he had not forgotten his promise to Susie and he had saved himself for her. When she had told him that he would find someone else, he rejected the idea instantly. If she wasn't going to make him happy, then no-one would.

Twenty five years later, here he was, alone in a flat with a tiny kitchenette and two bar fire. And a song that had the power to squeeze his reason from him.

Oh! Ruby!

"Oh, hello, Mrs Trent.

I say! This is just like old times isn't it? Queuing up together outside a shop. Yes, the note says that he'll be back in five minutes so we might as well wait. I feel like I should have my ration coupons in my hand though. Funny how you get straight back into old habits. Wouldn't that just put the tin lid on it if he'd run out of whatever we wanted when we got in the shop? We had some fun didn't we, back then.

Talking of shops, how is your Terence getting along at Woolworth's? Oh? Promotion already, up to the small appliances counter? Oh you must be proud, bless him. He was always such a hard worker. I remember when he did that paper round that time and spent all day getting it right. Perseverance. He has that in buckets doesn't he?

Aww my Billy? Yes. Now there's a tale. He gave us the run-around for a while over his choice of career. Arthur wanted to get him took on as an apprentice at his place, but he wouldn't have it. We kept on sitting him down and saying to him "Now Billy, you've got to choose something. You can't keep umming and ahhing for the rest of your days. You've got to decide on a job." But he kept saying "Don't rush me. I'm thinking." But he would not talk to us about what he was thinking. He was just like that man who works in the bank. Inscrutable.

Anyway, a few weeks back I was tidying out his room when I accidentally found these clippings from newspapers and magazines stashed at the very bottom of his sock drawer. They were all about this actress woman, Joyce Grensomething. And she was always dressed as a policewoman. So that night as were having our tea, I tackled him about it. Head on. I says to him "Billy, what's all these clippings in your sock drawer? Have you developed a crush? Because if you have you'd better stop it right now. No good comes of crushes on film stars, you look at your Auntie Sylvia, always mooning about round the back door of the theatre it's a wonder she hasn't got herself into trouble."

Well, he looks up from his pudding and he says to me "Ma, there's something you should know. I'm mad on Policewoman Ruby Gates. She's in the films, see, and I've been to the flicks to see her five times. And I've come to a decision. I'm joining the police force."

So I had to point out to him, Policewoman Ruby Gates doesn't serve on our local constabulary and if he thought that by joining up he was going to end up walking the beat with her then he was very much mistaken.

"Yes, I know that, Ma." He says "But she's made me see that joining the police is what I want to do. I want to work with people like her. And I think that a policewoman's uniform is just smashing."

"Well, at least you've come to a decision." I says to him "And you've certainly got the feet."

So that's what he's done. He's at training college now and I've had a postcard from him asking me to send more socks so he must be getting about.

Oh look, here we are, open again.
Nice to chat with you, Mrs Trent. No doubt see you at the Rose and Crown for Horace Parker's wedding do. Yes, I know. Third time lucky, that's what they say. Between you and me I've no idea how the other two stuck him as long as they did. He never shuts up."

Forgetting

Bob decided that he ought to marry Carol before her hemline got any shorter. If he put it off any longer, then she would start looking indecent and his mates would start laughing at him behind his back. At least if he lived with her, he could keep an eye on her.

They were both very young. Their blinking bedazzlement at their newly secured status of being grown up shone from their faces as they stood on the Town Hall steps. The photograph, taken at that very moment, was framed in brass and placed on top of the television set. They rented the television, and had to be careful that the frame didn't mark the wooden veneer. The settee and twin-tub washer were on H.P. What with the payments for these, the rent and the food there wasn't much left over at the end of the week. Especially when they had spent their traditional Friday night in the Prince of Wales. Carol found that she was no longer able to buy new clothes – so her hemlines remained steady at last year's level.

The lack of new clothes and shoes began to grieve Carol. When they first married, Bob had asked her to give up her job at the hosiery factory. He could keep them both, he assured her. They had got a small council flat with a nice kitchen for her. She could spend all her days there quite happily, eking out the housekeeping money and making the most of every bit of scrag end and potato that she could get her hands on. It was what his Mum did. Carol ought to spend a bit more time at Bob's Mum's house, he said. She could pick up a few tips. But Carol got tired of making do very quickly, both with the food and with her clothes. They were always wanting girls at the factory, indeed they had told her that she was welcome back again at any time. Her friends had wondered why she was leaving in the first place, when she wasn't even expecting. So one particularly lonely Tuesday afternoon, she went and got her old job back.

Carol explained it all to Bob as she served him a steak and kidney pudding. A special treat now that more money was going to be coming in. She wouldn't be bringing in nearly as much as he was, of course. But there would soon be enough to buy their own television instead of renting. And they might get a telephone installed.

"What do we need a telephone for? There's a box a few yards down the street."

Those were the only words that Bob spoke to her in response to her news. He scraped half of the pudding into the bin and then went to the pub without her. She had been happy until then, so sure he would see the sense in it.

Bob found two of the usual Friday crowd sat by the darts board. He slammed his pint down onto their table and sat astride a stool.

A gaunt faced old man offered Bob a roll-up as he rasped a greeting

"Ay ay, someone's not happy. And drinking on a work night! Had a row with the old lady then?"

Bob grunted. "She's decided to go back to work. Gone and got her old job back." He breathed out acrid smoke "Starts on Monday".

"Awww. Can't keep her at home then?"

The other man laughed shortly but looked over at Bob. "Can't see what's wrong with it myself. All the more money in your pocket, son."

"Yeah but next thing she'll be expecting me to do bits of stuff round the flat. And what about having my tea on the table when I get in? Going to have to wait for it now while she moans and groans about getting it ready."

"Well she can expect all she wants, can't she son? Don't mean you have to do it. Just relax, have 40 winks while she cooks the tea, know what I mean?"

Bob grunted again. He could see their point. But he didn't like it.
"My old Ma never worked. Dad always kept her and they've always been satisfied."

"Times is changing, mate. Let her out. It's more money in your back pocket if you don't have to keep her."

Carol was determined that this would work for them. She soon learned that it was best not to speak of work in an evening – not of anything that had happened and especially not of the others that worked there. She would rush in 15 minutes before Bob got home and ensure that his arrival was met with the preliminary smells of his tea. Shopping was done a little at a time during lunch breaks and the flat was thoroughly cleaned every Saturday afternoon. She bought a pair of shoes with her first week's wages, just to remind her of the reasons to keep going. She wore them without asking Bob if he liked them, and as his opinion was not sought it was not given.

Bob had in fact noticed the shoes, but he was determined that she would not speak of her work and that the products of it would go ignored. It irked him to have to wait for his tea, and Carol's frantic housework on a Saturday afternoon gave him a simmering sulkiness. He appeared to be spending more of his leisure time alone. It was during one of these lonely times that he got his big idea. It was an early evening and Carol had taken a bath. He lay on the sofa, watching television and filling his belly with custard creams. The box in the corner flickered and chattered. He screwed up the emptied packet of biscuits and drained his mug of Nescafe. There was nothing else to do but pay attention to the old woman who was being enthusiastically applauded on the screen. It was that Joyce Grenfell. His auntie had once done one of her speech things at the Christmas talent contest at the club. She was quite funny, putting on her posh voice. She had come third. This time, Joyce wasn't being that nursery school teacher that everyone went for and that his auntie had copied (now there was a thought….a nipper or two would keep her at home). No, this time she was being a woman singing in church, fretting because she'd left a gas ring on. Too much of an old busybody, rushing about, probably. Easily done when you've got a lot on your plate. Now there was another thought. A timeline of potential events popped like bubbles in his mind as he heard the water drain from the bathtub.

Bob began his campaign on a Wednesday evening. That was when Carol really started to look tired. She had a bit of a rest on Sundays and it got her through Mondays and Tuesdays. But she seemed to slacken off in the middle of the week. His tea was simpler and mainly involved bunging things into the oven. She had placed a pan of tinned peas onto the front right hand ring of the Belling this time. Bob was careful to notice this as he went into the kitchen on her call.

"Let's eat in the living room." He gathered up the cutlery and the cruet. He watched her dish up the food onto the plates, then with a rather clumsy manoeuvre he shepherded her into the next room. As he followed, he clicked the cooling hob ring back into an 'on' position, then pulled the kitchen door half closed behind him.

They ate in front of the television, the plates balanced on their drawn up knees. Bob finished his food first, and silently waited for Carol to put her knife and fork together. He half rose as soon as she had done so and lifted the plate from her lap.

"I'll take these through. Is there any pudding?"

"Yes, some Angel Delight in the fridge." She smiled at him, determined to encourage the smallest gesture of help.

He burst into the kitchen, a plate in each hand which were banged onto the draining board with a clatter.

"Carol! Come here!"

His voice was so serious and mustered such command that she went into the kitchen in a couple of bounds, a frown creasing her small features into a grimace. "Yes, love?"

"You've left the ring on! Look at it, it's glowing red hot!"

"But I'm sure I turned it off. I must have done. I always do."

"You can't have done, Carol. That ring is switched on full. Feel the heat coming off it. I've not just turned it on, have I?"

"Oh dear. I must have forgotten this time. How strange."

"Yes. Tired, aren't you?" He softened his voice.

"We're both very tired. I'm sorry if I made you jump. But even with all your extra money we can't afford to waste electricity like that."

"No, sorry. Let's get the Angel Delight and sit down again."

He smiled. "Alright." Then he left her in the kitchen, a pile of washing up before her and puzzlement in her mind.

Pleased with his success, Bob was tempted to construct another bout of mind absence for Carol. But he decided that a few days' gap was needed. If her memory went all at once, she might just put it down to the time of the month or something. So he hung back, but he plotted.

On the following week, Carol misplaced her hairbrush, only for it to appear again by the kitchen sink. A bath tap was left running on the week after that, although luckily for Carol the plug was not left in. A few days later, the imersion heater was left on all day. But still, it never occurred to Carol that she might need to slow down her pace of life by throwing in the job. Rather, she began to let the housework slide. Breakfast pots were piled by the sink and not washed until tea time in order to allow and extra ten minutes in bed. The duster and can of Mr Sheen seemed to disappear entirely. This was not what married life should be like, Bob was convinced. It was not what he was expecting.

After being regaled of a tale of a lost house key at work one day, Bob's great denouement was born. Carol left for work about ten minutes after he did. But if she were to suddenly have no key…well then, she wouldn't be able to leave at all. She would have no choice but to stay at home. On the Friday of that week, he waited until she was in the bathroom. The tap was running and she was scrubbing her teeth with some concentration. He went to her handbag, which she always left on the chair and deftly removed her bunch of keys. He placed them in the zip pocket of his jacket and then with a "cheerio, love" he left the flat, locking the door behind him. They were not yet connected to the telephone; she had no way of fetching him back.

He thought about her periodically throughout the day, at turns guilty and exhilarated. He fantasised of her falling into his arms when he got home, exhausted from the crying and hard thinking which had finally enabled her to reach the correct conclusion. It was with a simmering excitement that he reached the front door that evening. He unlocked it softly, stretching his head into the hall as he eased it open. He could hear the television playing plinky plonk music, while there was a faint smell of mince being reheated. Clasping Carol's set of keys firmly, he removed his hand from his pocket and placed them on the floor. Using the tip of his shoe, he pushed them underneath the hall stand, just out of sight. He breathed out, pushed the door to and breezed into the living room. Carol lay on the settee, watching the television and clasping a small velveteen cushion to her stomach. The chipped enamel bowl that she used to soak their underwear in lay empty on the floor.

"Hello." He was conscious of the need to give nothing away, but she did look pale. "You alright?"
Carol sat up, still clutching the velveteen cushion, and patted the seat next to her. "I've had a very funny day and I've been doing a lot of thinking."
"Oh yes?" He sat, willing himself not to say anything more.
"Just after you left this morning, I finished brushing my teeth and the next thing I knew I was sick everywhere. I just couldn't stop."
"Oh? Oh, so you've not been to work?" He had to make an effort not to sound dejected.

"No, I just crawled onto here and lay down for most of the day."

"Oh, I see. What's going to happen about tea, then?" Carol managed to tell Bob that yesterday's leftovers were in the oven for him before she began to delicately heave, clasping the metal bowl to her chin. She brought nothing up and lay back, exhausted by the effort.

"So what do you think caused it? Something you ate?" Bob thought back to what they had both eaten the day before. "What did you have that I didn't?"

"I don't think it's something I ate, Bob. My little visitor's about ten days late and I'm always on time. And all this forgetting things…well sometimes a woman's brain can get a bit addled…"

"What are you saying, Carol? Are you telling me you're expecting? What about taking the pill?"

"I must have forgotten one day. I think I'd better go and see the doctor tomorrow."

He smiled at her. "I hope that he says that you are expecting."

"Do you?"

He nodded, kissed her on the cheek and then went into the kitchen to take the plate out of the Belling. He began to whistle. He was going to get his wife back…

Some Ladies Have to Dance Together

"You could never win with my Dad. If you didn't do as you were told, you'd get a rollicking. Then it would be the silent treatment. Oh, he was a terrible sulker. And the atmosphere that came with it – that was the worst thing. It would feel awkward just passing him on the landing. And if you tried talking to him, he would either ignore you or come over all triumphant about it. Even as a child myself I could recognise the childishness in him. And even if you did do as you were told, he could still be horrid. He would revel in his control over you with songs, old jokes and rough play. Sometimes I felt like I had a blanket wrapped around me far too tightly, and I would start to panic that I couldn't escape it.

When I was about 14, I was allowed to start going to the school disco – though my Mum had to plead with him. It was always held on the last Friday of the month between seven and half past eight. I had to go with the girl that lived three doors down. We weren't in the same class and we hardly knew each other, but that was the condition of being let out. Dad would watch us go down the street together.

"Stick together." He told me. "I don't want to hear that you've been cavorting about with boys. Just have a dance and a gossip with your girlfriends." Yes he did actually use the word cavorting. He used to read The Sun newspaper, I expect he picked it up there. But the idea of my dancing with a boy really worried him. Looking back, I expect that he knew that when I took up with a boy, I would no longer be wholly his and that was something he just couldn't stand. He was ever so jealous over Mum, she couldn't even wear make-up.

So I would go to the disco and stick with the girls. We danced in a small circle sometimes, me and two or three others. If a boy approached me, I would laugh in his face and tell him to push off. I went home with a clear conscience but goodness knows what effect I had on their self-confidence. When I got home again, Dad would be there and every time it was the same thing. "Not been dancing with any boys, have you?" I'd tell him no, I'd just been hanging around with my usual friends, dancing with the girls. Then every time, without fail, he'd throw back his head and laugh and begin to sing...

"Stately as a galleon I sail across the floor, doing the military two step..."

It was torture. I was fourteen and he was singing this stupid old song about old hags dancing together at me at the top of his voice. I used to go straight up the stairs despising that Joyce Grenfell woman. I knew that if I said I had been dancing with boys I wouldn't have been allowed to go again though.

But you change very quickly at that age. It wasn't too long before I did start to want to start dancing with boys. After all, a lot of my friends were doing it. There was one boy in particular. He was in the year above me at school. One of my friends found out from his friend that he fancied me, so they got together and shut us in a stationery cupboard until we had agreed on a date. What we agreed on was to hang around together at the next disco. It was lovely, we danced all night and he gave me a bit of a kiss before we went home. When I got there, of course I had to keep it from Dad and I was a bit worried that he would somehow know. So when he sang his usual song I was a bit relieved really. As time went on, and my disco date got a bit heavier, well I got to the stage when I was glad to hear the song. It was the best thing because it meant I hadn't been found out and he hadn't spotted the snogging rash. I even began to hum along a bit.

Eventually, after I had escaped from home, hearing the song actually made me smile. It still does. I know all of the words."

Retirement Time

"Bobby! Bobby! Come here, there's a good boy. Now, Sam. You're a naughty boy. Come away from that nice lady with those muddy paws.

I'm awfully sorry about that, they do get so uncontrollably giddy when they are let off the leash. I do hope that he hasn't marked your coat. I have a damp hanky with me if he has. I find it a handy thing to have when we come for a trot near the marshes. Ah, here comes your doggie now, he's been for a rummage in the bushes, look!

Oh? He's a she? Delightful.

Bobby! Bobby! Don't do that.

I'm so sorry. He has been neutered.

Ah yes, I do seem familiar to a lot of people. You see, I was the local nursery school teacher for many,

many years and people do retain a vague recollection of me as they progress through life.

I'm awfully sorry but I so very rarely remember my pupils – so many have been through my hands and I only ever seem to remember the naughty ones.

Oh Sammy, you've brought me a lovely big stick. What a good boy! Here we are then. Catch!

What was your name, dear? Jenny? Jenny…No I so very rarely remember I am sorry. No. Wait a minute. Were you the little girl who used to forget to pull her knickers up when she had been to the toilet?

Ahhhh! There now! How lovely to see you again. You've taken to wearing trousers now I see, very sensible.

Bobby, do get down. Leave the poor little girl doggie alone.

Well that's all in the past now that I'm retired. No, I don't miss it at all. My doggies and I have a lovely peaceful time. There were some days when I felt that all I did was nag…

Well Jenny, I must go because it's nearly nap time. Off we go, little doggies."

20650148R00038

Printed in Great Britain
by Amazon